Abuelita's Paradise

Carmen Santiago Nodar
Illustrated by Diane Paterson

Available in Spanish as *El Paraíso de Abuelita*

Albert Whitman & Company,
Morton Grove, Illinois

Text © 1992 by Carmen Santiago Nodar.
Illustrations © 1992 by Diane Paterson.
Published in 1992 by Albert Whitman & Company,
6340 Oakton St., Morton Grove, Illinois 60053-2723.
Published simultaneously in Canada by General Publishing, Limited, Toronto.
All rights reserved. Printed in the U.S.A.
10 9 8 7 6 5 4 3 2 1

Library of Congress Cataloging-in-Publication Data
Nodar, Carmen Santiago.
Abuelita's paradise / Carmen Santiago Nodar ;
illustrated by Diane Paterson
p. cm.
Summary: Although her grandmother has died, Marita sits in Abuelita's rocking
chair and remembers the stories Abuelita told of life in Puerto Rico.
ISBN 0-8075-0129-8
[1. Puerto Rico–Fiction. 2. Death–Fiction. 3. Grandmothers–Fiction.]
I. Paterson, Diane, 1946- ill. II. Title.
PZ7.N6717Ab 1992   91-42330
[Fic]–dc20   CIP
                                                                    AC

*Dedicated with thanks and love to my
Colita, Abuelita, Mama, y Mommi–
four generations of grandmothers. C.S.N.*

For Grandma Cole. D.P.

Marita's father puts Abuelita's rocking chair in Marita's room.

"Your grandma, your *abuelita*, wanted you to have it,"
he says. It's covered with Abuelita's old fringed plaid blanket. Faded
letters on the blanket spell *paraíso,* paradise.

Marita holds the blanket and sits in her abuelita's rocking
chair and remembers the stories that her grandma told her.

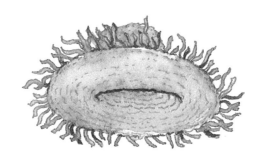

"I lived on a farm in Puerto Rico," Abuelita would say. "Up in the highlands, where butterflies fly. Where night creeps over the mountains and down again. Where sunlight sparkles the day, and sugarcane reaches the sky."

"Tell me more, Abuelita," Marita would say.

"Morning was still night when my father whispered, 'Wake up, *niñita*. Today's the day to see giants.'

"After breakfast I would run to the barn and get Pedrito and Pablito, our oxen. My father would hitch them to the cart and put on his *sombrero*. Then out to the fields we'd go."

"Did you wear a *sombrero*, too, Abuelita?"

"Yes, my father's old one."

Abuelita rested her head back, with eyes closed.

"What did the sugarcane fields look like?" asked Marita.

"They were tall, almost as tall as this house. When the trade winds blew, the plumes of the flowering sugarcane bowed and curtsied. They reached up like feathery angels, dancing and floating toward heaven. My father looked as if he had shrunk when he stood next to them; I looked like a little ant, he said. We would laugh, and he would tickle me and say, 'My little ant better be careful or the cane will eat her up!'"

"Could the cane eat you up, Abuelita?"

She opened her eyes, looked at Marita, and smiled.

"No, he was just teasing. I stood in the middle of the flowering cane. Then I held onto a bunch of swaying stalks and danced with them. I could hear cane falling as my father chopped with his *machete*. Then he called, '*Hijita*, my little daughter, come out!'"

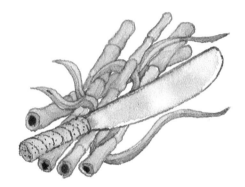

"Did you come out, Abuelita?"

"Yes, I did. But when my father cut the stalks I had danced with, I started to cry."

"And then what?"

"My father saw tears in my eyes and said, 'They will grow back. Look, the roots stay in the ground, and they will grow again next year. It's just like when Mommi cuts your hair–it grows back, doesn't it?'

"'Yes, Poppi,' I answered. He lifted me, we spun in a circle, and I hugged him tight.

"Later, I dragged the cane that lay like a sea of sticks and hay toward the cart. We worked until midday; then my father chopped a stalk into small chunks, and we sucked on them on our way home for *siesta*."

Marita cuddled closer to Abuelita. Abuelita touched Marita's face, and Marita kissed her hand.

"Did you sleep at *siesta* time?"

"No, I would wait and watch quietly."

"For what?"

"The honeycreeper bird. Every afternoon, from the clear blue sky, the honeycreeper flew in through the kitchen window. It came on a stream of light, looking for bits of sugar on the kitchen table."

"What did you do, Abuelita?"

"I tried to talk bird talk to it, but it ignored me."

"Did it stay long?"

"Just as long as it wanted to. It wasn't afraid."

"What else did you do when you were little like me, Abuelita?"

"I fed the chickens, and sometimes I plucked them."

"What's plucking?"

"Pulling the feathers off the chicken," Abuelita said. "Like this!"

Abuelita's fingers picked at Marita's tummy and around her neck. Marita folded over laughing and bumped heads with Abuelita, and they laughed even harder.

Marita asked, "Why did you pull the feathers off?"

"Because the chicken was dead, and my mother had to cook it."

"What did you do with the feathers?"

"Put them in a basket and saved them!"

"For what, Abuelita?"

"In the evening, as the sun went behind the mountains and night was starting, we would sit on the porch. My father played his lute, my mother stitched new pillow sacks from ticking, and I, with a basket of feathers, stuffed the sacks for pillows."

Abuelita pulled the blanket up to their necks.
"*Paraíso*," she murmured.
"Where is paradise, Abuelita?"

"My Puerto Rico – far, far away," she said. "Over the trees and across the ocean, there is an island that is home to me. Where castles and fortresses stand watch over the sea, and where, long ago, pirates on galleons came to plunder the land."

"Tell me more," Marita said.

Abuelita rocked and whispered, "Rain forest dew clung to me; trees, vines, wildflowers, and giant ferns surrounded me; tiny tree frogs sang, '*Coq-ui, coq-ui*'; and cool waterfalls made rainbows just for me."

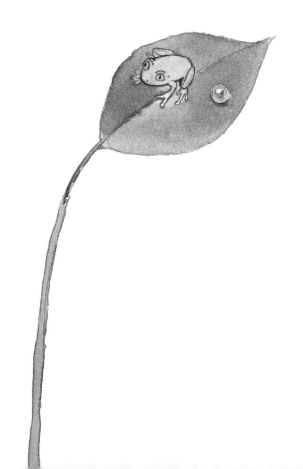

She closed her eyes and sighed.

"What else, Abuelita?" Marita asked.

"I would sit with my mother on our mule, and my father would lead us through winding roads, like horseshoe curves and mazes, into the woods. So long ago," she said. "But Puerto Rico will always be paradise to me."

Now alone, curled in Abuelita's chair, Marita can smell her, like roses in the garden.

She feels Abuelita's arms as she draws the blanket around herself. Marita rocks gently, and she can hear Abuelita say, "We're floating, flying high. We're birds soaring through the sky."

Abuelita rocks faster and says, "Hold on, we're on a wild man's ride!" They laugh and laugh and hug, and Abuelita laughs so hard that she cries.

Marita squeezes her tight. "I love you, Abuelita."

Abuelita strokes Marita's hair. "*Mi niñita, mi niñita* – my little girl, my little girl."

But Marita's abuelita is gone. She died.

Marita's mother comes into the room and sits with Marita in Abuelita's special chair. "Abuelita's in another paradise," she tells Marita. As they sit embraced, Abuelita embraces them both.

Marita says to her mother, "Someday, I'll fly in a plane. Over the trees and across the ocean, to see castles and fortresses, where pirates on galleons came. Where sugarcane reaches the sky and dances and bows and curtsies."

"Abuelita would have liked that," says Marita's mother.

"I'll walk through the forest feeling the dew, surrounded by trees, vines, wildflowers, and giant ferns. Tiny frogs will sing, '*Coqui, coqui.*' And cool waterfalls will make rainbows just for me."

"And then what?" asks her mother.

Marita rests her head on her mother and whispers, "On a mule, I'll travel winding roads, like horseshoe curves and mazes, into the woods. And then . . . "

Holding Abuelita's blanket close to her face, Marita falls asleep in her mother's arms and Abuelita's embrace.

NOV 18 1992

DATE DUE			
		Gabriella	